When Santa Claus Met Sandy Claws

A Cape Cod Christmas Story

To Rosie and Tavi –
Always Believe

Jim Wolf

– ENJOY!
ROSIE & TAVI
Anne Rosen

By Jim Wolf

Illustrations by Anne Rosen

To Begin With...

Every year on Cape Cod people want to hear a Christmas story. I try to find a new story to tell that will help mothers and fathers and grandparents and children all get into the spirit. Last year, I started to worry that I would not find one when, as often happens, some young friends decided to help me out. I was down in Provincetown, visiting with Nitara (she's ten) and her brother Tyler (he's nine). They sat me down on MacMillan Wharf out near the fishing boats, and told me a Christmas story about their family. Nitara said that there were certain things I should know before I listened to the story.

She told me that every year when Santa leaves the North Pole to fly around the world, he takes two sacks with him. One is full of toys, and one is empty. At each home, after he delivers the toys, he takes out the other sack and fills it with delicacies that the families have left for him— you know, the best things to eat from that part of the world. While Santa goes around the world, the toy sack gets emptier and emptier, and the delicacy sack gets fuller and fuller. When he finally comes back to the North Pole with his sleigh and eight tiny reindeer, he and Mrs. Claus and the elves sit down to a big feast with delicious food from all over the world. Nitara said that this was something I probably didn't know, even though I'm a storyteller!

The feast at the North Pole is 'traditional' for Santa, she said, which means that it happens every year. Tyler said it was 'traditional' just like clam pie for Christmas Eve dinner in their own family. Nitara said, "Uggggh!"

"It's one thing that we didn't really like about Christmas," Tyler said. "We had to eat clam pie. Mom makes it and we couldn't say we didn't like it 'cause on Christmas Eve if we said we didn't like something Mom cooked, Santa might hear and we might not get any presents!"

Nitara put her finger to her lips. "Shush, or you'll spoil the story, silly brother."

Tyler shushed.

1

Nitara and Tyler's Story

'Twas the night before Christmas in Provincetown Harbor, and the sun was going down, the sky was tinged with red, and the water was flat, like a pane of glass reflecting the sky and the twinkling lights from town. Russell the lobsterman was out in his boat, the Fish Tales, with his kids Nitara and Tyler. They were allowed to be out there with him because they were on school vacation, and because it was so very calm on the water that evening.

So, there they were, pulling up the last lobster pots for the last catch of the year, hoping they would make enough money to build a new bedroom. Usually, Russell did not work on Christmas Eve, but this was going to be a special winter. They were going to have a baby in the house soon.

Russell steered the boat very close to a buoy and put the line into the block and around the winch. Next, he flipped the switch and the winch creaked and squeaked as the pot came up from the bottom. Finally, he reached over the side to swing the pot into the boat where it smacked down on the deck. Nitara and Tyler pulled the lobsters out of the pot because, being the children of a lobsterman, they knew how to pick up a lobster without being pinched by those snapping claws.

Meanwhile, up at the North Pole, Santa was getting ready to go. The elves were all done with their work. They were tired and dusty with bits of sawdust in their hair from making toys. Mrs. Claus came over to Santa to give him his last instructions.

"Now, Santa," she said, "The elves have earned a fine reward this season. I want you to bring back the delicacies as you always do, but this year I want especially good ones!"

"Yes, dear, I'll bring back the finest delicacies," Santa promised. He kissed Mrs. Claus good-bye, climbed up into his sleigh, and then he and the reindeer were gone.

Back near Provincetown, right around Long Point, not that far off the shore, the Fish Tales was heading in.

"Did I ever tell you kids the story about your old Uncle Nick from up north?" Russell asked with a smile.

"Tell us, Dad," they said together. Russell always told good stories.

The sky was fading to dark, the lights on Pilgrim Monument were twinkling brightly, and there was only one more pot to be pulled up. Russell was just starting to tell them the story. That's when it happened.

You see, suddenly there was a streak of white, or maybe it was light. It was white and it was light and it went streaking across the sky that was not yet night— it was the man in the red and the white! Tyler and Nitara looked up and saw Santa with his reindeer and sleigh shooting above the world over Cape Cod Bay.

Santa's Arrival

Then the sleigh swooped down over the Fish Tales, and came in for a landing, right smack dab on top of the wheelhouse! Santa jumped off the sleigh and looked down at the three of them. They all looked up with their mouths wide open, even Russell, and he was a grown man! He had never expected anything like **THIS** to happen!

Santa chortled, "HO! HO! HO!" and jumped from the wheelhouse down to the deck.

Tyler whispered to his sister, "Did you see that! His belly IS just like a bowl full of jelly!"

"Yeah!" She whispered back.

Santa smiled at them. "What did you say, kids?"

"Nothin'!"

"I'm Santa Claus, in case you were wondering, and you—" He pointed a finger at Russell, "YOU! I want you to give me something!"

When Russell finally got his mouth working, he stammered, "Okay... uh... Santa."

Santa said, "Cap'n, I would like to take whatever is inside the last lobster pot you pull up back to the North Pole with me. Okay?"

Russell thought about it for a few moments. It was a hard decision to make, because he needed all the money he would get from selling each and every legal-sized lobster.

16

So Santa said, "Tell you what. I'll sweeten the POT for you. HO! HO! HO! Did you get that? I'll tell you what I'll throw in. If you give me the last lobster for my feast, I'll make sure that your kids— " Santa winked at Nitara and Tyler, "Nice looking kids— been good have they? I'll make sure to give them the best of all the presents that I've got in my sack. The best of 'em for your two kids if you give me the last lobster in the pot. Whadd'ya say?"

Russell looked at Nitara and Tyler and he knew that there was no way could he turn down **THIS** deal.

"Okay, Santa," he said, "Okay! What comes up in the last pot is yours."
They shook hands on it. Russell glided the Fish Tales over to the lobster
buoy and began hauling up the pot .

"OH! I've never felt one this heavy!" he groaned. "Nitara, come here! Tyler, you too. I want you to help me. Reach over and get a hold of it with me. Santa, you stay back and hang onto the kids if they start to go overboard. Okay now, no waves coming. Ready?

NOW! LET'S GO! HEAVE!" And they pulled as hard as they could.

Sandy's Arrival

They all stepped back and the lobster pot landed on the deck with a thump. A huge claw was sticking out of the pot. The claw was way bigger than Tyler's head!

"OH, MY!" shouted Santa, "That's a good one!"

Russell couldn't say anything at first. His mouth just hung open.

Santa asked, "Are the big ones rubbery and tough?"

"Well, I think they're just as good as the smaller ones if you cook 'em right," Russell finally said. "But I've never tried to eat one THAT big before!"

"Mrs. Claus and the elves are going to love eating this lobster," Santa chortled, as he hopped about the deck like a leprechaun.

"Just that claw alone could feed a navy!"

"Did you ever think," Santa continued, "what a perfect delicacy a lobster is for Christmas? When it comes out of the ocean, it's green and red. And then, after it's cooked, what color will it be?"

Russell and Tyler and Nitara all said, "Bright red!"

"My favorite color!" said Santa. "How perfect for a Christmas feast!" He licked his chops as if he could already taste it. His eyes rolled up at the sky. "Mmmmmm," said Santa. "I can't wait to dip lobster meat into melted butter!"

Russell aimed the spotlight at the pot to get a better look and they all peered inside. And then, all at once, everyone said, "OH MY GOODNESS GRACIOUS, WILL YOU LOOK AT THAT!"

The lobster was so big that it took up every inch of space in the pot.

It had a green beard that grew from its chin and wrapped around its shell. Over and over again the beard wrapped around, like a bald man who combs a couple of strands of hair to cover his shiny head.

"How many years do you think it took to grow a beard that long?" asked Nitara.

"He must be very old," said Tyler.

Just at that moment, a sound came from the pot... a voice as old as the hills... as old as the seas!

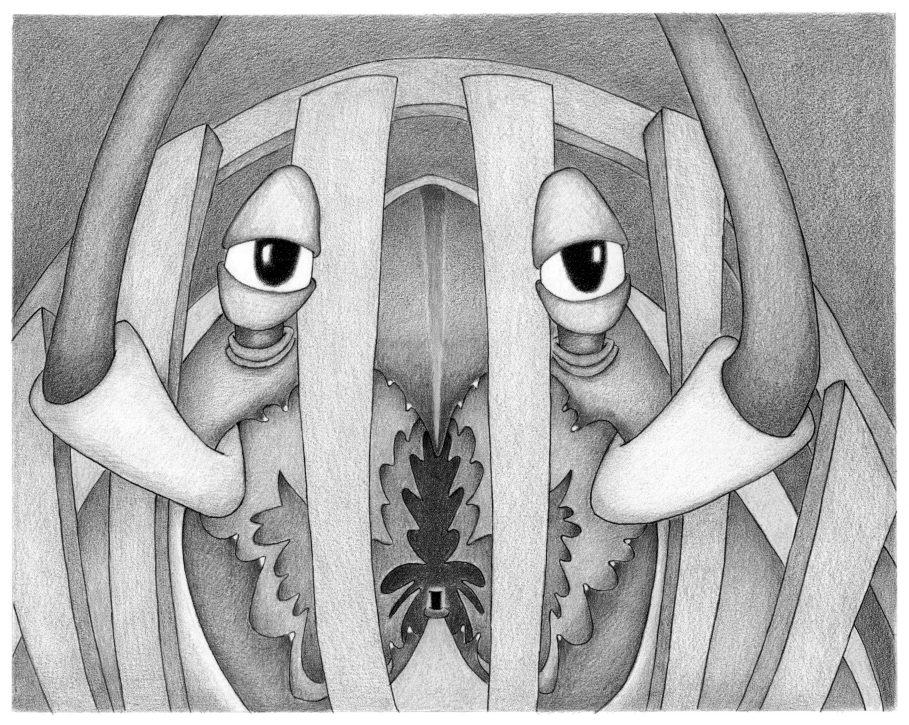

"I'm old, all right!" growled the voice, "Older than all four of you put together!"

"Who said that?" Nitara asked.

A reindeer snorted.

"I did!" said the lobster, "I'm one of the oldest individuals in the sea! I heard what you said, and I do NOT want to go up to the North Pole and become elf food! So you'd better listen to me!"

The lobster gazed at Russell with his two black eyes. "Lobsterman," he said, "I commend you on a great catch— ME! Now that you've caught me, how would you like to make a deal with me?"

"Another deal!" Russell said, "This seems to be a day for deals. What kind of deal do you want to make?"

"For my freedom, of course," bellowed the crustacean. "If you let me go, I will give you one wish. What do you wish for?"

Russell scratched his chin. "Well," he said, "To be perfectly honest, we have a new baby coming to our family soon, and I was thinking I shouldn't have made that deal with Santa. I was wishing that I could take you into town right now and sell you. No offense, but by the pound you're no ordinary paycheck."

"This is just my day," cried the lobster. "You want to sell me, and old jelly belly over here wants to eat me." He poked his claw at Santa's belly. "I'm stuck between a buck and a soft place."

Santa looked down at the old lobster and then at his tummy. "He might be too magical to eat," declared Santa. "Kinda like eatin' a reindeer. Wouldn't be right somehow. I can't do it!"

"So you won't be taking him home for your feast," Russell said. "If I give you something that's just as delicious as lobster, will you still give my kids the best presents in your sack?"

"Certainly," answered Santa, "But it better be especially good."

"Phew," sighed the lobster with great relief, "I'm NOT going to be eaten tonight... but Russell's wish is to sell me. Listen up! I have a better idea."

"Let's hear it," Russell said.

"Help me out of this pot and I'll tell you."

Sandy's Plan

Russell released the lobster onto the deck. There wasn't much left of the pot when he was done.

"Now," said the lobster, "Come close and I'll tell you what we'll do. Get this boat back to the wharf, and once we're there, put me inside Santa's empty sack and take me to a restaurant where people are eating their Christmas Eve dinners. Plunk the sack down on a table and say, 'Who wants to see Sandy Claws?' "

Russell almost choked. "Your name is Sandy Claws? Well! Blow me down! Sandy Claws, meet Santa Claus!"

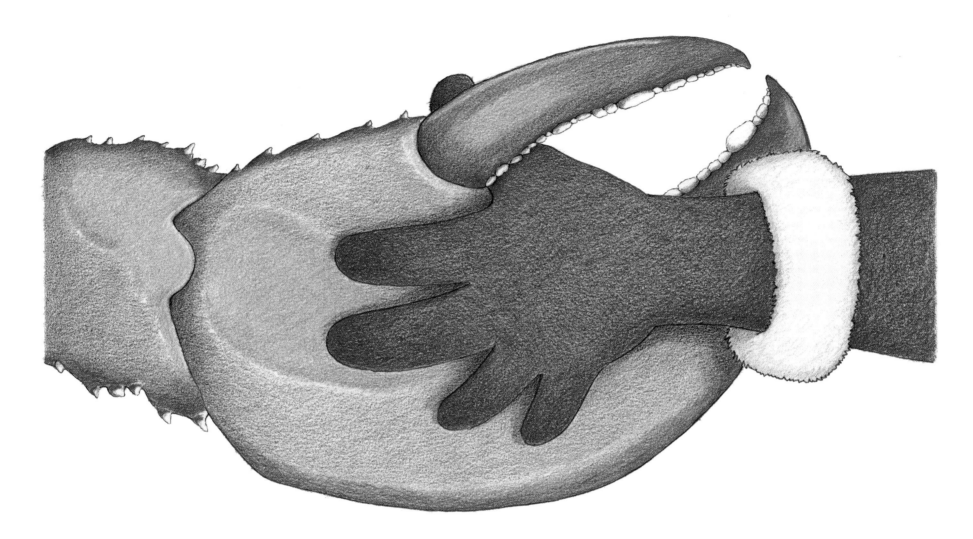

Santa reached down with his hand and Sandy reached up with his claw and they shook. Santa Claus and Sandy Claws!

Then Sandy Claws told the rest of the plan. "Take me to a restaurant and plunk me down on the table and say, 'Who wants to see Sandy Claws, a dollar a peek!'"

"OH! OH! OH!" exclaimed Nitara, "I wanna carry Sandy Claws."

"NO! ME! ME! ME!" shouted Tyler, "I wanna do it! I'm stronger than you are!"

"Listen up, you two youngsters," said Sandy Claws, "I weigh seventy pounds. Neither one of you can take me all by yourself. You're going to have to drag me together."

And so they all agreed on the plan.

"Listen, Cap'n," Santa said to Russell, "I gotta see this. I gotta see the people of Provincetown looking at this thing— 'Sandy Claws,' fer cryin' out loud, and thinking they're gonna get a look at me. So, whadd'ya say we trade clothes, and I'll go into town with your kids? I'll look like an old fisherman with your yellow slicker on and my pipe clenched in my teeth. Ha! Ha! Ha!, I mean, 'HO! HO! HO!' This will be a real hoot."

So Russell and Santa traded clothes. First, Santa put on the oil skins, and the yellow hat that was hanging on a hook in the wheelhouse.

"My wife Jamie will get a kick out of this," Russell chuckled. He put on the suit of red. It was a little short in the arms and legs, but there was plenty of room around the middle!

Pretty soon the Fish Tales was docked safely at MacMillan Wharf. The kids put Sandy Claws in the sack and set out with Santa following along.

Clomp, clomp, clomp went their rubber boots up the wharf to Commercial Street. They headed for the first restaurant they saw... The Lobster Pot.

A Dollar a Look

Tyler and Nitara dragged the red velvet sack into the dining room with Santa Claus right behind, puffing on his pipe, looking just like an old fisherman.

The place was full of people eating their Christmas Eve dinners. Everybody looked up and stared.

A man called out, "Hey, kids, what's in the sack? But first, who is the fisherman? He looks mighty familiar."

"Oh, him?" Nitara said, "Oh, he's our old uncle Nick. He's visiting from up north."

Santa Claus nodded, his pipe waggling between his teeth. He held out his hands with both thumbs up. "Waaaaaaaay up north," he said.

Tyler and Nitara picked up the big sack and plunked it down on a table between four people. "Guess what we caught in a lobster pot?" they asked the crowd.

Everyone was quiet.

"Can't guess? We'll tell you, then— Sandy Claws!" And they said it quickly so nobody could tell that they said "San-DY Claws". They said it all as one word, "SANDYCLAWS! In this sack right here! A dollar a look!"

Of course, the four people sitting at the table thought they should have a look. Other people started to crowd around, but the familiar-looking-fisherman-uncle-from-up-north, said, "Back to your tables! Back to your tables! One table at a time!"

"That'll be a dollar," said Tyler. "A dollar from each of you!" The customers eagerly put down their money. Nitara and Tyler opened the sack, and the four people at the table leaned in to get a look.

You could hear a pin drop in that restaurant. Then from inside the sack came a "HO! HO! HO!"

"Oh, My Goodness Gracious, will you look at that!"

Nitara scooped up the four dollars off the table and Tyler quickly closed the sack. They sped from table to table, and the money came rolling in.

"Oh, my goodness gracious, will you look at that!" everyone exclaimed. When Nitara and Tyler were done at The Lobster Pot, they moved on. From restaurant to restaurant they pulled that sack, until their pockets were stuffed with money.

Finally, Sandy Claws called out from inside the sack, "Back to the boat! And step on it! I'm getting CLAWStrophobia in here!"

"HO! HO! HO!" chuckled Santa, "That's a good one!"

"You should have thought of claustrophobia before you climbed into my dad's pot," said Tyler. "What were you doing in there?"

"I was taking a nap," said Sandy. "It's very restful inside a pot. Safe from enemies. As long as you don't get pulled up!"

"And brought to a POT luck supper," Nitara giggled.

Santa's Reward

Back at the wharf, a few townspeople stood looking out towards the Fish Tales. They were stretching their eyeballs trying to see what was glowing on top of the wheelhouse. One said to another, "Will you look at what Russell did on top of his boat this year! If that's not the best Santa's sleigh and reindeer I've ever seen! I wonder how he made it look so real."

The kids just walked right on by, dragging the sack, not saying a word. "Sure is a fine Christmas display," commented the familiar-looking fisherman as he passed by, puffing on his pipe. "Those reindeer are fine looking animals."

Meanwhile, Russell had been mighty busy. He walked right through town in Santa's red suit, to his little house, where he crept in the kitchen door. Jamie was at the stove, just taking you-know-what kind of pies out of the oven.

As she placed the pies on top of the stove, Russell snuck up behind her and said, "Mmmm! That smells good!"

Jamie jumped about a foot into the air but when she turned and saw him, she laughed. "HO! HO! HO! I love your outfit, Russell. Does Santa know about this?"

"Of course he knows, my dear, it was his idea!" said Russell. "Those clam pies sure look great. I hate to do this to you, darlin', but do you think I could take the pies and give them to someone who wants them very much?"

"But Russell, my sweetheart, if you take the clam pies, what will we have for Christmas Eve dinner?"

"Jamie, my darlin', why don't you make your famous pizza, and decorate it with basil to make it green and red— a Christmas pizza! The kids will be as happy as clams!

"That's a great idea," Jamie said. "But please hurry back because I'm not making pizza all by myself."

"It will be our new tradition," he said. "I'll be back in a flash with the kids. We'll all help make the pizza."

So Russell carried the steaming clam pies through the streets of Provincetown, back to MacMillan Wharf and the Fish Tales. They were all there waiting for him— Tyler, Nitara, the miniature sleigh and eight tiny reindeer, and Santa, and Sandy.

"Whadd'ya got there?" sniffed Santa, eyeing the pies.

"Clam pies, Santa! Baked locally for your Christmas feast!" replied Russell.

"They look awfully good," Santa said. "Smell good, too. I'll take 'em!"

"I think that's a wonderful idea," said Nitara with a great big smile.

"Take the pies, PLEASE!" said Tyler.

Sandy Goes Home

Nitara and Tyler handed Russell the dollar bills. "Look at all the money we got from showing Sandy Claws!"

"Good job, kids! That will sure help pay for the baby's new bedroom," said Russell.

"Is everybody happy?" asked Sandy Claws.

"We sure are! We're getting a new baby, and Santa's best presents, too!" Nitara exclaimed.

"By the way, Dad," asked Tyler, "What's for dinner?"

"It's going to be pizza tonight!" Russell smiled.

"Yahoo!" said Nitara.

"Not clam pizza?" asked Tyler, worried.

"You never know..." joked Russell.

"Just so long as it isn't lobster," said Sandy Claws. "It's time for me to go back into the water before I dry up. An ancient lobster gets to go back to his home! That's what it's all about, you know. You fishermen should always leave some of us, especially the old smart ones. Somebody's got to tell stories to the youngsters. They'll all want to hear about the time I met and was almost 'et' by Santa Claus!"

54

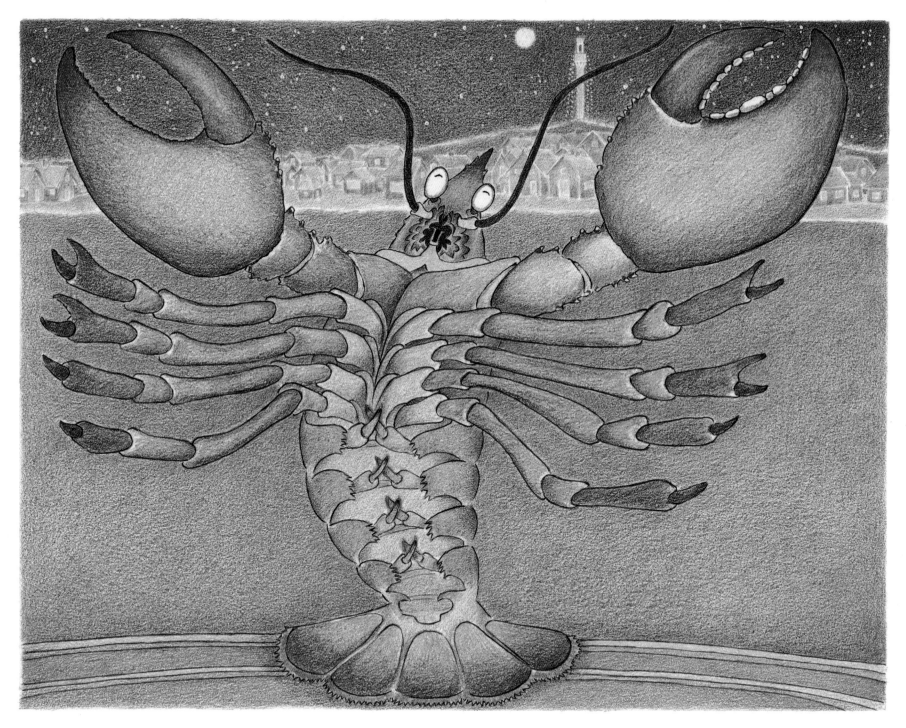

Sandy did a back flip and two
somersaults in mid-air and landed with
a great splash in Provincetown Harbor.

He swam all the way down to the bottom, still singing, not to be seen by human eyes again that Christmas Eve.

After All

And that is the story of what happened last Christmas Eve, when Santa Claus met Sandy Claws— at least according to Tyler and Nitara, my good friends from Provincetown, way down at the end of Cape Cod.

As we were walking back from MacMillan Wharf, Nitara said, "Dad told us it was a good story, but we shouldn't be surprised if nobody believes it."

"YOU believe it, don't you Jim?" asked Tyler.

"Well now," I said, "I suppose it could be true."

"And you'll come over for some Christmas Eve pizza this year, won't you?" asked Nitara.

"I couldn't pass up a thing like that," I said.

And what about you? Do you Believe?

Provincetown Clam Pie

Courtesy of Nancy Meads

2 cups chopped clams

1/4 cup butter

1/4 cup flour

1 cup milk

1/2 cup clam liquid

1/4 cup light cream

2 tablespoons chopped scallions

2 tablespoons chopped parsley

pinch salt

pepper to taste

pastry for 9 inch 2-crust pie

Melt butter in medium sauce pan. Whisk flour, milk, and clam juice, stirring to avoid lumps.
Add cream and stir until thickened over low heat. Add scallions, parsley, clams, salt, and pepper.
Pour filling into bottom crust in pie pan, cover top with top crust and crimp edges.
Bake forty minutes in a 400 degree oven.

Enjoy!